Short Stories

Robin Miller

ISBN 979-8-89345-505-2 (paperback)
ISBN 979-8-89345-506-9 (digital)

Christian Faith Publishing
832 Park Avenue
Meadville, PA 16335
www.christianfaithpublishing.com

Printed in the United States of America

On the Ride Home

Contents

Introduction

This collection of short stories is a look
into the musings of the author.

While we look not at the things which are seen, but at the
things which are not seen: for the things which are seen are
temporal; but the things which are not seen are eternal.

—2 Corinthians 4:18 KJV

Knock Knock

"That is so annoying!"

"What is?"

"Them calling you and you not answering. Why don't you answer when they call you? They know you are in here." She said it casually as she crossed over in front of me.

"They don't know that I can hear them, and as long as I don't answer, they won't know," I said with an inward mean streak. "I hate it out there. Why do you think I'm in here?"

"Because of my company," she said with a wicked tinge that she tried to withhold from me.

We both heard a knock and looked at one another. She looked at me with surprise, and I looked at her with recognition. "Who is that?" She hissed. She only hissed when she was mad or afraid.

"It's the man my parents asked to watch over me in the hospital. He won't come in unless I invite him, so most of the time I just speak to him from here."

"Well, get rid of him! He makes me nervous." She was hissing again, and I could tell she meant what she said.

"Don't worry. He won't come in unless I invite him, and I never do. I just talk to him at the door."

"Just him being around makes me uncomfortable. I'm moving." She moved further into the room, and I went to the door to speak with my visitor. He was nice, peaceful, and always had one question for me—was I ready for my healing? He didn't disappoint.

"Hello, Eve," he said.

"Hello," I replied simply.

"Are you ready for your healing?" I considered his repeated question and answered truthfully.

"I am afraid."

"Afraid? I will be with you. You will never be alone. There is nothing you will face that I won't be there with you."

"That is what you say, but I am afraid of the outside world. People have mistreated me, lied to me, and…"

"I know," he said with understanding.

"I don't want to ever go there again." I started to sob, and he held me. This was a first in our meetings. He was so full of peace that I almost changed my mind. I broke away from him and went to walk away.

"Your parents want you back very much. They love and miss you."

"I know. I hear them talking in my hospital room. Sometimes I want to answer them to let them know I'm all right and that they do not have to worry about me." I wanted to sob again, but I resisted the urge. Being around him was making me want to change my mind about hiding away in this room. Maybe I could live in this world with his help. I heard a hissing noise and remembered my friend. I would have to leave her. I wasn't ready to do that.

"Eve, you have but to ask, and you can be healed, surrounded by people who love you and will work with you toward your continued success."

I could feel myself wavering and wanted to cut this visit short.

"I'm not ready," I said flatly.

"I will come again tomorrow," he said gently, then left.

As he left, I heard my parents asking, "Doctor, how long will she be in this coma?"

"There is no medical reason for the coma. Her body is fine. It is strictly up to her when she wants to come out of it. I suggest you keep speaking to her and showing love. Medical science has substantiated that a comatose person can hear."

My mother moved closer, stroked my head, then kissed my forehead, saying, "We are waiting for you, baby. Come back to us soon."

A tear rolled down my face, and she wiped it away.

I turned away from the outside world and yelled for my friend, "Delusion!"

"What!" She hissed.

"He's gone."

"You mean Jesus?"

"Yes, I mean Jesus. He is gone; you can come out now."

"Why does He come uninvited?"

"My parents pray for Him to help me. So He comes every day to give me an opportunity to leave the confines of my mind."

"But you won't, will you?" She had a malicious tone I had not heard before. It sounded unfriendly and made me feel uneasy. I thought I had better tell her what she wanted to hear with only the two of us here.

"No, of course not. The outside world is too scary for me."

"Good!" She said. We walked deeper into my mind, so far that my parents' voices sounded like an echo. I looked at her—she seemed different somehow. Not as beautiful as before Jesus's visit. I think I may listen to Him more next time because being alone with her isn't fun anymore. It was starting to feel scary, and that was what I was running away from. I think the next time, I am going to invite Jesus in. I've denied Him for so long; I hope He accepts my invitation.

Simply Yes

"So what are you going to do?" I asked him. He puffed on the cigar, blew out the fire of the match with ashen-colored smoke, and took another deep drag of his cigar, exhaling the smoke into the room.

"There is nothing for me to do. She isn't my case, and by law, I cannot touch her. He won't listen no matter how many reasons I give him; they are dismissed."

He smiled, but I could tell that he was seething on the inside. A deep cough came from the patient's room. I was indignant. "Listen to that. She is ready to go, and you can't touch her!"

"I can't touch her," he said slowly, deliberately reiterating his previous point.

A haggard cough came from the opposite end of the hall. He smiled, showing yellow. "She is legally mine, and I can touch her."

"So why don't you?" I asked.

"And cut her suffering? Surely, you jest!"

We sat there until he had just about finished his cigar, listening to the woman hack and struggle for breath. "How is she yours and the other is not? The coughing woman never said 'yes' to you."

"She never said 'yes' to anyone," he answered. "By default, not saying yes puts her legally at my disposal." He smiled again, showing even more yellow than before.

I could hear the woman's breathing becoming ragged, and she fought for each one she was able to grasp. I could imagine her lungs aching from not being able to fill them with air. He stood up to leave the room. "Death," I said. "Are you going to get her?" He turned around and showed every yellow fang behind his lips, with smoke still billowing from the corners of his mouth.

"Yes," he said with relish. I almost felt sorry for the human. It was only a wink of time before he was gone, but I knew where he was by her screams of defiance, "No! No! Nooooo!" When will they learn that not saying yes to Jesus is the same as saying no to Him? I left the room to attend to my own cases. After all, I had a job to do too. Misery doesn't just happen; it needs my touch—the touch of Despair.

A Prism's Eye View

"Farez (Fleshman), what are you doing here, disconnected from your human? They are not asleep nor has their spirit been summoned by the Master."

I looked at him and could still hear the words of the preacher echoing as I separated from that time and that space: "The flesh don't wanna die!"

He stared at me and saw something; at least I saw something in his eyes. "What do you see in me, my Mentor?"

"I see rage and sorrow," he said in a simple response.

"Of course, I'm angry! Of course, I don't want to die! That is all they say in the churches as they read from the Holy Scriptures, but what they fail to understand is that I remember the garden. I remember being in a place of absolute peace and absolute beauty, in the presence of the Master, as I housed and walked the spirit of my Keeper through the garden, in the lush gift of their existence. The smells—ah, the smells! The humans believe if they leave the city and go to a remote place to smell the sea or the woods, it smells 'clean.' I remember smelling pure air—not pure from the absence of pollution, but pure because it was the very essence of the garden. Organic foods pale in comparison. The taste of the garden wasn't because it was untouched by man, but because it was touched by the Master. The delicate foliage that brushed against every cell of me, without the barrier of clothes or shoes or makeup or chemicals or any of these things the Keepers dress us up in today. I wish to go back there, but I am cursed to return to the dust. My mentor, this wasn't always so! Every part of me remembers and longs for that place." I sunk my head down and silently cried, mourning an end that was never supposed to be mine. "What can I do now but fight for each breath? Each moment, I can survive here because I cannot be there."

"What has become of your Keeper?" My mentor looked at me. I knew he wasn't dismissing what I had just said, but he could not offer me the comfort I desperately grasped for.

"My Keeper, my spirit man, remains in the House of the LORD, becoming ever more elated that she will receive a new body when the Master calls her home." I sniffled without meaning to. Her great joy was my great sorrow. Why did Adam do this to our kind? We would have hosted him forever without sickness, without ailments, without weakness, and without secret diseases that would come alive in him and cause his separation from this part of life. I looked down at my hands and saw the past—how the blood could be seen traveling in my veins. What a marvel the Master is!

"You must go back now," my Mentor quietly said. The sound of his voice jerked me back to the present, and I saw the thick covering that hid all the miracles of GOD underneath.

"I know. I don't know how to rid myself of this sorrow or the absence of peace I constantly feel."

"You cannot. The curse places all those things in you. Your Keeper is able to overcome those feelings with the power of the Master's Spirit residing with them in you. Go back and embrace His presence for the time you have." His words gave me hope and the will to return. "Farez, do not come here again unless your human is asleep or the Master calls her spirit home. You do harm as a host to your Keeper by behaving in this manner."

"My mentor," I said with heaviness in my voice, "she separated from me. It was the Word that ignited her so that I woke up here."

He smiled at me. "Then return in peace."

I floated away, moving closer and closer to the rejoicing hosts until I saw my Keeper still reveling in the joy of the Word. I connected back to her and, for a moment, felt a tinge of sorrow. I guess she feels my pain too. Then I felt a portion of her joy and looked through her eyes. I could see the Master! He cares.

Homeless

The wind was blowing through the trees and the leaves, swirling everything around, making it look like waves in the water. This was one of my few pleasures before night came. I wafted over the sidewalk and saw a familiar face in a not-so-familiar place, outside of his host.

"She kicked you out again," I said in a knowing question.

"Yes," he said, "but we both know it is only temporary." If I didn't know he was right, I would have told him he was pathetic. Going and coming back again. Sheesh!

"So what was it this time?" I didn't ask if he had gone too far because he always does. Her breaking point seemed to move further and further to the right, where he was concerned. He was going to be the death of her one day. I shuddered at the thought.

"Same ol', same ol'. She keeps trying to move beyond me, and then she lets me back in. I don't quibble; I just return when beckoned and pick up where we left off."

"Don't you think she is going to wise up to you?" I asked.

"Not if she continues to do the same thing, go to the same places, and keep the same company." He snickered as if he had said a joke.

"How can you do something differently if you keep doing the same thing?"

He shuddered. "It's cold out here. I hope she beckons me back quickly. I like it when I'm warm and comfortable." A waft of smoke drifted our way. He breathed deeply and rocked on the balls of his feet from the intoxication.

"It's her," he said in a throaty whisper, almost choked by his own excitement.

"How do you know it's her?"

"Do you think I've been with her all this time and not know her essence? The sorrow in her exhaled smoke as she breathes in the drug to forget the past and exist only in the now? It is her. She's using again." He began to move past me quickly with urgency. "I have to get to her while there is still an open door, or I'll be stuck in this void until the next time. I need to feel the warmth of a body again." He was so intoxicated, I wondered who was more high—she from the drug or him from the thought of exploiting her again.

As he moved past me, he called, "Come with me." He continued to move, and I stood still.

He turned while wafting backward, and he smiled. "You won't get this invitation from me again."

I snuffed. "Invitation? Destroyer, we both know you can't invite me in. The human host has to. It isn't your decision."

"Yes, but you are forgetting spiritual law; she has created an open door. Any one of us can come in—that is the invitation. It is so much easier to walk through an open door than to wait to be invited in, wouldn't you say, Suicide?"

He had a point. I wouldn't have to wait until Destroyer was through with her to work my luscious whims on her.

"I'm coming!"

We hurriedly floated over the sidewalk to reach her. Destroyer flew in a zigzag pattern, drunk with the smoke of her essence and the thought of being outside of this void, and back with his former human host. I was behind him, but I imagined his fangs were dripping with anticipation.

We arrived at her neighborhood. She was a grown woman and kept returning to the place of her hurt—her sadness. Humans are strange creatures. "Why does she continue to return here if she hurt so badly?" I asked Destroyer.

"Because she never left it. In her mind, she is always here. You can thank our friend Delusion for that!"

We were here. Now I could sense her spirit and was becoming heady from the sheer delight of ravishing this human, who was in the image of my enemy.

Lost in my revelry, I didn't see it coming. Something struck Destroyer and me so hard we reeled back. I lost sight of her for a moment.

It was a warring angel of my enemy! "You shall not pass to her." His voice sounded like many waters, and I was afraid to return an answer. Destroyer, drunk with the potential conquest of this human, spewed out in hatred: "She opened a door for me to return! She is legally mine!"

We moved forward, and the angel raised his sword again. As drunk as Destroyer was, he wasn't a fool. We stopped. "She is protected by the prayers of her grandmother and the saints. While they continue to apply the blood of the Savior, she is protected by Him. You shall not pass!" He raised his sword higher to solidify his words and looked at us with burning precision. His gaze felt like he was already slashing me into pieces.

Destroyer railed, spat, and cursed, but he did not move closer to the girl. He wafted backward in his rantings and then shot away. I followed him. The night was coming. There would be other open doors. I followed him, knowing he would know where to find them. Hopefully, we won't encounter any more angelic beings. He took away my high!

Learning from Experience

The student sat in the aisle seat with the intention of making a quick escape after class was over. He didn't want to be there anyway. The indignancy of being made to take a remedial course at his advanced level of practice. Pah! Another student squeezed past his drawn-up legs and sat in the auditorium-style seat next to him.

"Is this your first time in this class?" He asked him.

The student snuffed in disgust, answering, "No. I didn't recognize the condition of my case and was sent back to this class."

"Me too," said his new partner in the class.

"The way they act, you'd think it was life or death. I still achieved the required result. Why do I need to be here?"

A slam from the front of the room brought everyone to attention. The professor used a microphone to adjust his volume above the room noise.

"It is life or death," he said. "The end does not justify the means. You need to be able to correctly recognize the condition of your cases and bring them to an expected end using tested, tried, and predictable means." He turned away from his students and pointed a remote at the projector. A movie clip started with a woman sitting in her living room. She crossed her legs, then changed and crossed the other leg. She looked at the TV, then stood up and went into the kitchen to get a cup of coffee. Returning to the living room, she sat down, adjusted her seat, and then returned to the kitchen for a snack. She heated a muffin in the microwave, pacing as she waited for the timer to sound the familiar *bing*. She kept going back and forth, not getting adjusted nor enjoying the show playing on her set. The professor paused the clip and turned to his class.

"What is the condition of the woman? Why is she so jittery?"

The class was silent for a few minutes. The student sitting in the aisle seat raised his hand. The professor invited his answer, "Yes?"

"She is unsettled, nervous."

"So," the professor pressed, "what condition does that indicate?"

"That she does not have peace. She is unable to sit in calmness or enjoy her surroundings, though they are familiar to her. She keeps trying to appease herself with food and drinks."

"Very good!" The professor praised. "And what else does her condition indicate? Who is present with her, working on her as a case?"

"Thief. He has stolen her peace." The student in the aisle seat completed his answer.

"You are batting one hundred, Mr. Pride. Let's see if the others are paying attention. If Thievery has stolen her peace, who else can he invite to help him with his case?"

The student next to Pride raised his hand and said, "I wouldn't need anyone else to help me. She is in such a pitiful state I could take her down alone."

"Mr. Boastful, that is why you were sent back to this class. She has not hit rock bottom and would be able to resist you. Pay attention and learn!" The student shrank in his seat, embarrassed by the rebuke.

"Mr. Pride, perhaps you can enlighten us. Who would you invite to assist with this case?"

Pride looked sideways at his fellow classmate and sat straighter in his chair, relishing the positive attention of the professor. He started off with a lilt in his voice, as if it were obvious. "Professor Destroyer, I would ask Despair to help. He would undermine her hope."

"Good, but too far," the professor said frankly. Pride looked sideways again at Boastful and saw him snickering at his failure. He deflated but tried not to let him see.

"Going directly to Despair would push the human too far and have them regroup before you could mortally wound them spiritually. The correct answer is Confusion. It is the natural progression to the loss of peace; then Despair to weaken their hope."

The professor continued to expand on the lesson: "Pushing the human too soon and too far will cause them to rebound by calling upon their Master and reaching out to their prayer groups, but if you push lightly, you can convince them they are hearing your suggestions as their own voice. You only have the power of suggestion until you can legally claim them. Slowly, move them to your territory in a manner they wouldn't notice. A different choice here; a small lie there; staying too long in a place they normally wouldn't go for an 'innocent' reason, like a bridal shower or a retirement party. Before they realize how far they have moved, you have attacked and mastered their habits."

The bell rang, prompting laptop lids to be hurriedly shut and bookbags to be zipped closed. The professor stated above the commotion, "Students, read chapter 2. We will continue our discussion on the power of persuasion in our next class."

Pride and Boastful walked out of the classroom together. "Do you believe humans are that gullible?" Pride asked Boastful. "Sure are!" he said excitedly. "I can get a human to believe anything as long as I know they are listening."

"How do you know they are listening?" Pride asked.

"You know they are listening because they return to the same thought you planted. When they aren't listening, they dismiss it and start thinking about other things. Those that are in love with their Master begin to think on His Word." They both shuddered at this thought. Neither one liked working with cases that involved humans who loved their Master. That thought was enough to sober them and cause them to walk in silence back to their dorm rooms.

The Calling of the Birds

The fog rolled in, needling through the branches of the trees and infusing the side of the mountain with a light gray midst. It came with such force that some of it billowed upward, looking like smoke wafting into the night sky. A bird descended in a circle around the top of the cabin. Another squawked in a call, causing others to join in the swirl, flying above the cabin in a circular fashion. The mother continued to adjust her daughter's appearance. "Mommy, I hear the birds."

The mom answered gently, "I hear them too. That is our sign. It's time to get to work," the mommy said, smiling at her daughter. "I want you to follow me and do as I do. I'm going to teach you what you need to know to do Mommy's job one day. You are going to learn how to exercise faith."

The girl perked up with excitement. "Okay, Mommy!"

"Follow me." The girl followed her mother down the hallway as she stopped at the entrance of the bedroom. A man was sleeping in the bed. "Wait right here and watch me. I am going to stir up his faith."

"Okay!" The girl answered with continued excitement. The woman entered the room, knelt toward the man's ear, and began to whisper affirmations.

"The night has come," she said.

"*The night has come*," he repeated.

"I'm in the darkness," she said.

"*I'm in the darkness*," he repeated.

"I'm going to die!" she said.

"*I'm going to die!*" he repeated. The man began to softly moan and turn his head from side to side in dismay, shifting uncomfortably in his sleep. The woman stirred next to him and looked at her husband. For a moment, she recoiled, taken aback with a tinge of fear, believing her husband was going to die. Then she heard something on the inside: *I am a child of the King.* A flash of indignation shone in her eyes. She lifted herself up on one elbow, placed her other hand on the forehead of her husband, and prayed aloud with stern authority, "Spirit, you have no right to my husband. We are the children of the Most High King. In Jesus's name, you take your hands off my husband. Sickness, leave!"

The spirit was struck so violently that she flew backward, beyond her daughter, into the next room. Her daughter looked with dreadful awe at the huge, illuminated angel floating above the couple with a drawn sword at the head of their bed. The man roused, opening his eyes. He looked at his wife, gazing at him. He said, "I had the most terrible dream." His voice was shaking as he continued, "I was dying, floating out of here and away from you. I felt weak and powerless, but I heard your voice saying the name of Jesus, and I felt strength come back into me." The wife allowed tears to flow lightly from her eyes and kissed her husband on the cheek. They lay in each other's arms, praying and thanking God for lifting the darkness.

The girl both marveled at what she saw and dreaded what she saw at the same time. After realizing she had been captivated, she stirred herself and rushed to her mother. "Mommy, what happened! Are you all right? Why didn't the man's faith work?"

Sickness shook herself and stood upright, getting a good look at the angel that had bested her. She peered at him with searing hatred before answering her daughter reluctantly with the truth. "Disease, his faith did work. What we do is turn their faith upside down from their Master's Word. We plant subtle suggestions and make them think they are their own thoughts. Instead of faith to believe in wholeness, health, and restoration, we use their faith to make them believe they will die before their Master has planned for them to go home or allow them to settle for less than His best by convincing them to live with infirmity." She laughed wickedly, forgetting for a moment the angel in the next room. "What human in their right mind would live with Sickness?"

"But they do, Mommy, they do! We have been here for a long time!"

"I know, my dear Disease. I will figure out a way to wear him down so that you can get hold of him and never let him go!"

"I will, Mommy! I'll hold him tight, just like you taught me to."

The mother looked down with a pleased look, placed her hand under the daughter's chin to raise it slightly to her, and said in a lowered voice, "Right now, we must leave. The old woman remembered who she was, and it interrupted our plans. We'll go and come back. For now, the birds are calling, and others hear them too. We may be able to make another home tonight and have it along with this one. Would you like that?" Disease shook her head, yes. They both floated upward while warily eyeing the angel standing guard over the couple. Disease wouldn't tell her mother, but she could feel the heat of the angel's sword as they drifted away. Sickness cringed at hearing the couple's words of praise and adoration for their Master. She didn't tell Disease, but she felt they needed to find a new home immediately. They would not be tolerated here anymore.

Do You Hear What I See?

The teacher and the protégé leaned over the balcony to observe the people in the church. It was what the teacher had seen often, but today it wasn't his vision he was concerned about; it was that of his protégé, the novice learning what he needed to see. The preacher had been standing at the podium for nearly ten minutes—enough time for the choir to be seated, the ushers to return to their vantage seats, and the congregation to nestle in to attentively hear the Word of God. The Scripture was read, and the preacher began with passion to explain it and bring it forward from the past of two thousand years to make it current to today's believers. Enough time had passed. The teacher directed his protégé to close his eyes and explain what he was hearing. He could have closed his eyes, but he knew this was an exercise for him to learn a lasting lesson, so he veiled his eyes with two wings. He listened for nearly a minute and said to his teacher, "I heard the Word of our Master being taught to these people. The pastor is talking about the kingdom of our Lord."

"Very good. Now, cover your ears and tell me what you see?"

With two wings, he covered his ears—one on each side. He could no longer hear anything the preacher or anyone else was saying. He scanned from the back of the congregation to the pastor. When his eyes rested on the pastor, they widened from the sight. He saw little seeds being pelted out of the pastor's mouth toward the congregation. He was so enthralled he forgot his teacher's instructions and removed his wings from his ears, ready to exclaim to his teacher what he had just witnessed. When he did so, the seeds disappeared, and he heard words again. He was utterly surprised. He turned to his teacher to share what had just happened and hoped for an explanation of what he had just experienced.

The teacher already had a smile on his face before hearing the pupil's story. "Teacher, what just happened? One moment, I hear the preacher, then the next moment, I see black pitted seeds pelting from his mouth, then I hear him again. I don't understand."

The teacher answered with a serious tone in his voice and a smile on his face, "The seeds are the Word of God being planted in the hearts of man. You see in the spirit what is happening to the people when our Master's Words go out. Now look at the people and tell me, what else do you see?"

The protégé began looking more intensely at the crowd. He saw fellow angels and enemies in the midst of them. Demons were stealing the Word of God right out of the hearts of men! The seeds had sprouts but no roots as they were pulled out, pulsing with life from the different hearts—women, men, children, ministers, choir members—it didn't matter where he looked; no one appeared to be immune. His initial reaction was to fly by the side of the humans and protect them; he was stopped by his teacher's arm, which blocked his path.

"Teacher! Do you see this?"

"Yes," he replied. "I also hear nothing from humans to prevent it. They must command us. We do not work against their will, as our Master, does not work against their will."

The protégé focused his eyes on a married couple. He looked closely; the woman was dressed beautifully in traditional Sunday garb, as well as her husband. The two children, twin boys, were engrossed in a video game. Three demons were nestled by the family, one with the children, who looked bored since they were distracted by their video game, and one with the wife, who constantly whispered in her ear. Each time the demon whispered, she took her eyes off the pastor and peered at her husband with a frown on her face. The seeds hit her chest and ricocheted off. The husband appeared engrossed in the Word, but the seeds also ricocheted off his chest too. The protégé was confused by this sight and scanned the husband to see what he had missed. The demon was covering his ears. As he looked again, the husband looked like he was straining to hear the Word instead of being engrossed in it.

He felt his teacher stirring beside him and broke his glance from the couple to see the teacher's ears intensely alert and listening. A prayer wafted past them as it ascended: "Father, change my stony heart into a heart of flesh and put Your Word in it." They heard the command! They now have permission! As soon as the lowly soul finished their prayer, the teacher flew like an arrow between them and the demon that was snatching the seeds from their hearts. Their talons were in the process of moving forward to snatch the falling seeds when the angel's hot sword nearly cut them off. The demon didn't have time to attack but fell backward into a nearby comrade. They both stood and began to draw their swords when reality hit them about where they were, as more angels surrounded them in this holy place. Then, as if prompted, more humans began to pray, and more hot swords were flashing around them. The heat of their swords grew around the church with the believers' prayers. The demons growled to save their pride and floated away without pulling their swords.

The teacher said, "This is why you must watch and wait, but never impose." They did not return to the balcony. They stayed with the lowly soul, whose prayer began the revival and whose tears of humility watered the seeds being planted in their hearts.

Misdirection

"Juicy! Another round here!" the dark man yelled over his shoulder. The bartender looked over the rim of her glasses and rolled her thickly lashed eyes. The dark man continued speaking to his companion, seated across the round table from him. "You are a small business owner with a strong reputation in our community. You can really impact and be a part of the change in this neighborhood. Help families."

The businessman looked at the dark man and commented, "That's my hope. I grew up in this community."

"I read that in the news story they did about you. Are you in the same house you grew up in?"

"No," he said.

The bartender arrived with their drinks. She placed a short glass halfway filled with a bronze-colored drink on a napkin in front of the dark man. The ice cubes swirled in it and made a tinkling sound against the glass as she set it down. She placed a napkin in front of the businessman and deposited an ice-filled glass on it. Then she placed a can of diet cherry Dr. Pepper next to it. She pulled a straw from her apron pocket and laid it down next to his pop. She saw the pack of cigarettes on the table next to the dark man and stated, "Gentlemen, there is no smoking in this establishment. Will there be anything else?"

"No, thank you," answered the businessman.

"No," said the dark man. She turned and went back to attend to the bar.

The businessman continued, "When I was younger, I used to walk past a house on my block while walking to school. I thought it was so much better than the apartment my family lived in; it looked huge, had its own yard, and the neighbors couldn't hear what was happening in your house by listening through the walls. I promised myself two things: I would never be broke when I grew up, and I'd buy that house when I got older. That's just what I did." He popped open the can and poured his drink over the ice, causing it to make the same tinkling sound as his companion's drink.

"That's what I'm talking about! Help others to do what you did to duplicate that success. My firm reviewed your business practices and found you could be more profitable, pay greater wages, and provide more subsistence to families by having your employees work longer hours and mandate overtime."

"I read your proposal before agreeing to this meeting. The figures certainly looked promising. I wouldn't have to change anything but my hours of operation. That seems too simple." He eyed him over his drink as he asked, "And what do you get out of this?" He was preparing himself to hear the word *shareholder*.

"I know. I thought the same thing when my staff compiled the numbers, but I checked the data myself. It is that simple. Hey, I know you are thinking that is a lot to ask of your employees, but you will be providing a lot back to them."

"And?"

The dark man turned serious: "And I will get the fallout. When Daddy isn't home and his family is missing him, voila! Instant human capital for my own endeavors. They won't have a reason to be home when there is nothing to remain home for—you'll have your staff, and I'll have more for mine. That's it—all I want is the family." He smiled compellingly and then quickly added, "Working. No ties to you on paper; just a handshake agreement. What'd you say?"

The businessman sipped his pop before answering, "I will meet with my staff and get back with you. It sounds too good to be true, but if we can turn profits around and make it mutually beneficial at the same time, I am strongly leaning toward saying yes."

"Take some time, but not too long. You don't want to lose the advantage of the market. I would not be able to stand by the numbers provided, and a new workup would be necessary."

The businessman stood, outstretching his hand to the dark man. "I understand and appreciate this recommendation. It could be the answer I've been praying for." The dark man jerked back at this last statement.

The businessman looked at him quizzically as the dark man said, "My bad. You shocked me."

"Oh," said the businessman, laughing. He grabbed his hat and put on his coat. He reached into his wallet to pay for the drink.

The dark man raised his hand to stop the gesture. "It's on me. My thanks for your time."

"My treat the next time," the businessman said, putting on his hat. He turned to go, walking out the door. The dark man looked in the corner of the doorway and gave a nod to a figure waiting there. The figure gave a nod of acknowledgment back and followed the businessman out the door.

The bartender came over and sat in the seat vacated by the businessman. She helped herself to a cigarette from the pack lying on the table, lit it, and blew out the smoke while asking her burning question to the dark man, "Did you get what you wanted?"

"I will," he said through the newly formed cloud of smoke. "He is on the hook. I love when they fool themselves into thinking something good will come from backdoor deals."

"Destroyer, who do you have following him?" she asked.

"Greed. I need him to reinforce the money he could make to get his eyes off anything else that may distract him from saying yes."

She became emboldened and spoke her thoughts: "Are you sure this can work? Last time, we were run out by the prayers of the saints in the neighborhood."

Her mention of their last defeat soured the taste of his drink in his mouth, and he lashed out at her, "Remember to whom you speak!" He looked at her sternly and said, "Rebellion, just make sure you are in place to influence their daughters and their sons in the absence of their fathers. Their children will be the key to breaking down the family."

"Don't worry. I already have plans for those lovely darlings; such potential!" With that thought, she dragged long and hard on her cigarette, being intoxicated by her thoughts. At the same time, they heard a glass-shattering shriek. They were both startled and went for their swords. Greed staggered through the wall and fell to the floor.

"Greed! What happened?" said Destroyer.

He gurgled as he tried to speak. "I followed him, my general, as you commanded. I reached his house and was still keeping him preoccupied with the thought of all the money he would be making. I felt a premonition, but it was too late; I was struck mightily. When I opened my eyes, I saw two things—the angel that struck me and his wife praying on her knees in their bedroom. I fled for safety. My general, I fear you will have to abandon this plan. She has placed a covering over him. I could not penetrate their household." Greed lay on the floor, continuing to gurgle and wince from his wounds.

Destroyer and Rebellion returned to their seats. After a long silence, Destroyer spoke, "Call everyone up. We will have to regroup. He already has a hedge of protection. What we do outside is likely to be undone by his wife, coaxed on by the enemy, on the inside."

Rebellion asked, "Do you want me to send the scout to survey the adjacent neighborhood?"

"Yes," he said reluctantly, now sulking and starting to seethe. He tried to return to his drink, but his entire drink turned sour and would no longer satisfy him.

Father Knows Best

The wife scowled at her husband as the engine in the minivan started with a strong *vroom*! All morning, the family had been bickering and fussing over: where is my tie; Mom, is breakfast ready; I spilled juice on my pants; I can't find my jacket; there is a run in my stockings; why didn't you make the coffee; whose turn is it to drive; I need an offering for Sunday school; the hairdryer stopped and my hair is still wet; someone still needs to walk the dog; and many other quibbles. Everyone was on edge as they finally piled into the van and sat silently, angrily, for a ride to church, where they would, of course, be arriving late! The wife looked at the husband and continued to scowl. "Why did you let the car start? We had them at each other's throats. All you had to do was sabotage the engine. Now, you let the van start so that they could go to church. What were you thinking?"

The husband didn't allow her to rouse a reaction out of him. Instead, he smiled and surveyed his family, who were sitting in the vehicle with him.

"My darling, Delusion," he began, "it is your job to attend to the family, and it is my job to keep the family. You have done well with all the little foxes that have bitten their heels and sending them to church in a state that they will be unable to receive the word of their Master. Now, it will be my job as Illusion to put on a show for their church friends, and then it will be our son's job to keep the pretense going, believing the lie and not having repented to allow the Word to do a perfect work in their hearts. They'll just be 'going to church,' like they always do, with the thought that they did 'something.' You see, my beautiful bride, your hard work hasn't been wasted."

She cozied up to her husband and cooed at him, "My dear Illusion, you are brilliant! It is no wonder why we are a power couple in this region. Pretense, tell your father how great he is."

The teenager pretended to beam at his dad and said, "You're the best!"

The silence of the van was broken by the radio noise. "Please turn on service," the woman said with dry politeness. The channel tuned to YouTube as the preacher continued to read the Scripture, "If you have aught against your brother, leave your gift at the altar and be reconciled to him." The van came to a stop at the curb with everyone looking at the father.

He looked at his wife and began slowly, "Honey, I'm sorry. I don't know what got into me this morning. You are great to our family, and I apologize to you and our children. Everyone, please forgive me."

Delusion turned to her husband and began railing on him, "I told you it was a bad idea for them to hear the Word! Do you see what has happened? A whole morning of work is down the drain. Pretense, tell your father how lousy he is."

With sincerity, the teenager belted out, "You're the worst, Pop!" The human family was led in prayer by their father, leaving Illusion, Delusion, and Pretense on the side of the road as the family started back on their way to church.

On Vacation

She gasped and wheezed as she stumbled through the street. The button of her blouse had been dislodged from her scratching and clawing, trying to get relief from her painful heaving to get enough oxygen into her lungs. With disheveled hair and ragged clothes, she continued to drag herself to the next person. A man was holding himself up by standing against the stoplight pole. Seeing him gave her a splinter of hope; as hurriedly as she could, she made herself to him. Without salutation or ceremony, she grabbed the lapels of the man's shirt and hoarsely screamed, "Have you seen him?" Then she demanded, "Where is he?"

The man barely heard her. His attention was focused on not falling for the urgency of her grabbing him. He gained his composure and looked at her with milky-white eyes. He responded with little energy and stone-facedness, "When you find him, let me know."

She continued forward, driven by the thought of finding this no-good thief who chose to allude her in her time of need. "Jerk!" She yelled to the sky. "May the devil take him!" Her wounds began seeping again, and her chest hurt almost unbearably. If she could find him, she could get the relief she wanted so badly. She kept going until she stumbled against the curb and fell. She was motionless for a few moments to allow the pain to subside. Crawling to pull herself up, she sat in the grass against a car. The sun was searing hot. Nothing was a comfort to her—not the hot metal of the car against her back or the dry, prickly grass under her legs, and now stinging insects were coming for her weeping wounds. She smelled something burning. "Oh, great! Another thing to deal with!" She sniffed suspiciously and realized it was cigar smoke as a shadowy figure came from around the car.

A sinister voice addressed her, "Heard you been looking for me." She looked up at a wicked smile. She perked up, never thinking she would want him in her company.

"Yes! Please, I'm hurting real bad. I need you to fix me up. Make it so that I can leave here. I can't stand it anymore!" Her voice began shaking and shrieking into a psychotic tone.

He began toying with her, "I don't know. You never wanted me in your presence before, especially when the darkness came. You were always afraid and prayed I wouldn't come around. Now you want me to help you feel better?" He laughed at her suffering and continued to taunt her. "Not so high and mighty now, are we? Yeah, I could make all the pain go away, but I won't." He dragged slowly on his cigar, knowing what she would do next—they were all the same, pathetically the same.

"Please, I'll give you anything; I'll do anything! Just help me escape this pain."

He laughed in her face and began to walk away. "I'm just enjoying the view. I can't. I'm on vacation. I'll see you when all of this is over." He continued moving away from her, leaving a billowing trail of smoke.

Her screams blended in with the other cries, "Death! I hate you! I *hate* you! Come back here and take me from this life! I hate you! Don't leave me!" He moved through the streets, being scintillated by the suffering of the humans instead of his cigar.

Trouble

The man saddled himself onto the bar stool and sat limply over the counter. "Whiskey sour," he said, looking down at the marbled top. A few moments later, a glass appeared with a clear liquid that burned, going down the gentleman's throat as he drank it.

"Woman trouble?" The bartender asked, busying himself by wiping the counter around the customer.

"You could say that," the man replied as he continued nursing the glass, drinking down the contents in slow, deliberate gulps. He continued to open up to the barkeep: "No matter what I do, I can't get her to focus on me. I create a distraction. Nothing! I mess with her car. Nothing! I even show up at her job. Still, nothing!" The customer slammed his drink onto the counter, causing it to slosh out of the glass and giving the bartender more to do. "Sorry, Mac."

The bartender wiped up the spill and was thankful for the pause. He didn't know what to say. Most of the time, the men that came in with women trouble had gotten caught cheating; this poor fool couldn't even get noticed. "Well, now. Have you tried presenting the lady with what she loves the most—say, something for her children or a trinket that has a connection with her family?"

"I tried connecting to her through her family first, but she wouldn't hear of it."

"You've got it bad. What do you plan to do about it?" The bartender stepped away and returned with a fresh order to replace the customer's nearly finished drink.

"I'm at a loss. How do you get the attention of a lady? She wants for nothing and is content, so I haven't been able to wedge into her life like others that came before her. Doesn't she know who I am?" The customer began to sit straighter on his barstool and raise his voice. "People respect me for being able to make or break them. I can turn a life upside down with my presence, my influence, and my power. She doesn't know who she is dealing with!" The bartender looked at the slowly burning anger of the customer, who was agitated into his self-aggrandizing monologue.

"You don't have to tell me, Sir. I've seen you here with others before. Why waste so much time and energy on this one? Why not go back to the others who received you with open arms? What makes this lady so special?"

He enunciated with bitter hatred dripping from each word, "She. Rejected. Me." He continued, "I won't let her get away with that. Who does she think she is? She isn't better than any other woman I've dealt with." He stood up to leave. His glass was empty, and his resolve was restored. "I'm going to double my efforts. I'm missing something."

He turned to leave and looked back over his shoulder at the bartender's response. "Good luck!"

"I don't need luck; I need to keep at it, at her. Thanks, Mac." He put a tip in the oversized glass mason jar on the counter.

"Thank you; uh, I didn't get your name."

"Aekar."

The bartender repeated his name with contemplation, "*Aekar.* That sounds foreign."

The customer snickered and said, "It depends on where you are from; that is my natural language. It is Hebrew."

"Really? It is my understanding that Hebrew names are chosen for their meanings. What does it mean?"

The customer walked to the door as if he didn't hear the question. He stopped before turning the doorknob to leave and said over his shoulder, "It means *trouble.*" He walked through the door, leaving the bartender suddenly moved to pray for the woman they had just been talking about.

One Chance

"Come forward!" The man at the podium called as a sign for the princess to move ahead. The young lady was attired in a long white lace dress with the insignia of the royal family on her headdress.

"My Lady," her attendant by her side broke into her thoughts. "Are you sure you want to do this? Perhaps you want to wait until a more opportune time, like during a national emergency."

"No. Now is the time. I am ready," she said as she moved forward.

The large, deep-chested man behind the podium spoke again. "Your attendant will have to wait here." Before her attendant could protest leaving his lady's side, she raised her hand in agreement. The deep-chested man turned, and she followed him down a long hallway. Stopping abruptly, he turned around to address her. "Remember the rules: you have one question within your lifetime to ask the ancestors. One question, one response. Going beyond these doors will be your only opportunity. Are you prepared to move forward, or do you choose to turn around?" He stared at her without blinking to receive her answer. She looked past him and studied the doors for a moment, then looked back into his unblinking eyes and nodded yes. "My Lady," it was the first time he recognized her title, "are you sure you want to move forward?" She continued looking at him and nodded yes again. "You may remain as long as you want; you may speak as long as you like, but you have one question to ask and one response to receive. Once that has happened, you must leave, never to return until you bring your successor to exercise their one question. Do you understand?" With all the humility she could muster at his childlike questioning, she nodded yes.

He turned and opened the double doors, stepping aside for her to enter. She walked past the ceiling-to-floor double doors and entered the dimly lit room. The doors closed behind her with a hollow sound. She stood where she was to allow her eyes to adjust to the low light. In the middle of the room, there was a chair. *Such a grand entrance for a humble room*, she thought. She made her way to the chair and sat on its edge with one foot crossed behind her ankle and her hands folded in her lap. Even during her nervousness, she practiced being poised, exemplifying her royal heritage. She studied the room. The double doors remained behind her, with two windowless walls on either side of her. The wall in front of her displayed an abstract painting. She was certain that if she looked at it long enough, it would begin to resemble something in her mind's eye.

She stared at the painting for a few moments and wondered what to do next. She called out, "Ancestors?" No answer. She called louder, "Ancestors?" Perhaps she should look at the painting longer. She had been taught that they were mirrors that reflected the soul of a man. She looked longer and thought she saw something on the side of the painting. The wall seemed to be moving. It was fading away, leaving the painting floating in midair. She felt like she was dreaming. Bit by bit, piece by piece, the wall dissolved away around the picture, and then finally the picture dissolved too, leaving a black chasm. She continued to sit straight in her chair, ankles crossed, hands clasped, and folded in her lap. Now, she decided to call again. "Ancestors?" Her voice floated beyond the room, into the chasm, and echoed back to her, sounding like a multitude. She stiffened at the ominous echo.

Peering into the chasm, shapes started to appear. It looked like floating people were coming toward her. Like a dream, they moved closer and were many. One was in the shape of a man with snow-white hair, a woolen garb, and a staff. He looked like he had lived many years ago. Another was of a lady who looked elegant with curls upon curls pinned on top of her head, powdery makeup, and long lace about her figure. Another, to her astonishment, looked like a child, adorned with a five-pointed crown about his head and regal clothes on his person.

One after another, the shapes filled the gap in the wall: old, young, male, and female. One caught her particular interest—he was girded about with a loincloth only, long locks past his shoulders and down his back. The remnants of chains were around his wrists, but not connected. His muscles had seen hard labor, and his face had seen the weathering of the sun. Yet it still held compassion. A woman in tattered clothes on her vestige followed behind him, holding the outline of an infant. As her eyes moved from them to those around him, she could see the wall was filled with the outlines of her ancestors—some she knew, some she did not recognize as family. She remained silent, waiting for their instructions. With one voice, with their lips moving in unison, they broke the silence. "One question, one response." The sound was low and thundered across the room to her ears. Their eyes were fixed on her. This was the moment. She breathed out a steadying sigh.

"My ancestors," she began, "since the time of my youth, I have been trained to be the ruler of my country. I have been educated on history, taught how to speak, royal culture, critical thinking, stratagems of war." She continued, "I have been trained in many things and taught that I must die as a sacrifice if necessary for my country. In all these things, I have not been taught how to serve my country or how to serve the people. My ancestors, my question is this: I know how to sacrifice and die for my country; how do I live for my country?" For the space of an hour, there was no sound, only the hovering eyes of her ancestors looking back at her. Finally, the eldest spoke without the others joining him in unison. Only his lips moved.

"My daughter, you have asked a hard thing. With the many things our lives could tell you, we can only give you one response: Go with God." After saying that, all began dissolving back into the black void of the chasm. She desperately wanted to yell, *Wait!* But she knew if she did, it would dishonor her ancestors and this sacred ritual. As she mused over her answer, the walls returned, bit by bit, piece by piece, and lastly, the painting. It did not appear as it had left. Now, the painting was boldly inscribed, *Go with God*. Not knowing if she should touch it, she stood, turned around, and walked out.

When she arrived at the end of the hall, her attendant and the large man who led her there were waiting for her. They both bowed, "My lady." She nodded her acceptance in return and left with her attendant. All the way back, she mused, *Go with GOD*. What did that mean? She tried to feel, to convince herself as if she were further along in her journey to know how to govern her people and how to serve them, but she was not. She was left with a puzzle instead of her answer, *Go with GOD*. The princess arrived back at her palace. Normally, she would stop to admire the majesty of the building, but today, her mind was still in the room she had just left. A servant broke into her revelry, "My Lady."

She started slightly at the greeting and managed to allow for more, "Yes?"

"A package arrived for you ahead of your return. It has been placed in your royal chambers."

"Thank you," she said, nodding her head in acceptance of the servant's message. The servant bowed and left her presence. *A package?* she thought to herself. She went into her chambers and saw it on her dressing table exactly as the servant informed her. It was wrapped in purple linen with a royal blue bow tied on the outside. A notecard was under the bow with the king's signet. How strange! Her father had passed six months prior; how could this contain the royal seal of his ring? She rushed to open the card. It read, *My Lady, your ancestors could only give you one answer. To guide you, they gave you The Answer.* She turned the card over and continued reading, "I am Alpha and Omega, the beginning and the ending, saith the Lord, which is, and which was, and which is to come, the Almighty." (Revelation 1:8) She laid the notecard down and unwrapped the package. It was the painting! She read it again: *Go with GOD*. Tears flowed down her face. She now understood how to lead her people with the comfort that she had access to every answer she would need to govern them. Her ancestors gave her all she needed to walk through her life's journey. She would indeed *go with GOD*.

Plus One

"Morality is for those who can't afford anything else." The room erupted in laughter as the woman cozied up to her husband, pleased with the response of her guests. Her husband hugged the arm that was linked over the crook of his elbow and mirrored the same acceptance for his wife's comment.

"Absolutely right, dear," he cooed to her. "It's those religious nuts who have to find happiness in their God. If I want happiness, I find it at the helm of my yacht, in the private seat of my plane, or wherever I choose to be when I don't want to be here. I am not limited in my circumstances."

"Here! Here!" the room echoed.

Encouraged by the positive responses, he continued. "I am not stuck in my reality. I can create my own reality. They are stuck in their own minds with imbecilic thinking."

"True! Absolutely! Poor fools!" came the round of responses. The husband and wife sat at the table and indulged in the admiration of the intimate crowd. A still small voice came from the corner of the room, set apart from the rest of the guests. "What do you do in times of storm?"

The husband looked around the room to identify its source. He rested on a woman dressed in a smart, crisp white pantsuit with silver stiletto heels. Her hair was pinned in a bun, and he could see her eyes, clear and without reserve, in the presentation of her question. "Well?" She sipped Perrier water with cherries from a straw as she eyed him, expecting an answer. The atmosphere of the room shifted from her question, with all eyes looking with expectation toward the husband.

He felt the shift and made use of his hesitancy to come up with a question for her response. "What do you mean, in times of storm? Haven't you heard, money answereth all things?" Once again, the crowd laughed with him, and he breathed an inward sigh of relief. Who is this woman to challenge him? He was the host! The guest was undeterred by the room and the levity of his answer, in an attempt to dismiss her question.

"I mean," she started, "the water isn't always calm enough to go yachting, the sky isn't always clear enough to fly, and money doesn't change the weather. Those 'religious idiots,' as you label them, aren't bound by their circumstances. How do you handle not being able to leave *your* circumstances?" The silence from her question was awkward. It was turning the evening too serious for the hosts and the guests.

The host avoided the question by accusing her, "You must be one of them. Are you?" She sipped from her straw with a smile.

It was her turn to use levity to answer his question: "I didn't think you were into labels. I thought you said they were for the weak-minded." The room laughed at the unexpected comment, causing the host's cheeks to redden. "I'm just saying, what do you do? They appear to have an answer to that question."

The host kept it light, feeling as though he were losing the argument and being bested in his own home. "For the wealthy, there is always an out. You just have to have the right lawyer." He winked his eye, and the room was in favor of him again.

He was saved when a cabin steward interrupted with the clarion call, "Dinner is served." The guests filed into the dining cabin. The husband and wife were the last to leave the room.

They looked at each other with the same question in their eyes: "Who invited her?" In the corner of the room, an angel leaned comfortably against the wall. A demon looked, seething. Speaking in a restrained voice, the demon asked, "How did you get in here? You have no legal right. This is my domain."

"The woman was invited; I have a legal right to accompany her. She carries the spirit of my Master."

"Stay in your place, little angel, or you may find your wings clipped," the demon barked out. The angel smiled without offering a response. He knew the demon was limited to threats. His assignment was protected by the Almighty. He almost felt sorry for him. He knew the woman would not keep quiet. He floated toward her in the dining cabin. The rest of this night was going to be interesting!

Hearing the Silence

"Listen closely when the process starts; you must not say anything or ask any questions. Do not interrupt the witness's statement. Doing so will taint the evidence and discontinue the statement from the witness. It is imperative that you follow these rules for the sake of the victim. This is a highly unorthodox procedure, and any questions you have should be asked of me now. Do you understand?" The doctor looked directly at the intern and waited for the answer to the floating question. The intern looked back at the doctor and nodded yes without uttering a word.

They both turned and looked at the young woman in front of them. She was dressed in a pale ivory silk dress cut in trumpet couture, which accented her curves. Her makeup was modest, along with her jewelry. She accented her attire with diamond-stud earrings. The only eye-catcher was her primly curled hair and a stunning tennis bracelet accenting her left wrist. The intern wondered about a handbag when the doctor came alongside to give a reminder of what would happen next. "The lights will be turned off to dim the room and remove any distractions. The only light will be on the patient. It will seem really dark at first, but as we receive the statement, your eyes will adjust. Are you ready?" The intern turned a gaze from the patient to the doctor and nodded again, not trusting to speak during such an important process. One that would speak for the witness and bring justice for her.

"All right then, we are ready." The doctor turned off the general lighting for the room and turned on the patient lighting. It funneled around the patient and illuminated her ivory silk dress. She looked beautiful. The intern almost broke the silence, lost in the beauty of the woman and the thought of how harm could have come to her. The doctor's voice broke into the intern's musings.

"Miss Doe," the doctor said authoritatively as he took a step closer to the patient. "Miss Jane Doe. How did you arrive here in this examination room?" They waited. Soon, they heard a poised voice accented with irritation.

"My name," she began, "is not 'Miss Doe.' It is Cerebella O'Cinni of the Vangeller household. I came here to visit my cousins abroad and take a sabbatical before my impending vows. In my family, the tradition of arranged marriages is still honored." No one spoke as they continued to listen to the beautifully dressed woman. "How did I arrive here?" There was a pause before she continued. "I was invited to attend a socialite party with my cousin. She convinced me to go by telling me, 'It will be loads of fun!' My curiosity got the best of me. Parties at home are so…not fun. They are usually for the politicians to schmooze, so I agreed to go. I did not know my cousin had dates set up for us. One was her friend, and the other was her friend's brother. I turned into the 'extra' with an 'extra.' We made the best of it by talking and even had a few dances together. I wasn't very interested in it and wanted to leave. My cousin, on the other hand, was very much enjoying the party and her date. Me leaving would put an end to both for her, so I stayed.

"The longer I spent with my date, the more he started hinting at us being alone. I was offended by his innuendos. I am a pledged woman and was keeping company with him, not truly dating him. His last 'suggestion' was the final straw. I abruptly walked away and spoke to my cousin to inform her that I was leaving alone if I had to. She asked for five more minutes. It wasn't unreasonable, so I granted it. I left them alone to say their goodbyes. My date approached me and asked why I was leaving. Fed up with his arrogance to suggest being alone with someone he didn't know and wasn't his fiancé, I told him. He was angry and yelled insults at me. I wasn't going to stay for that! I began walking down toward the parked limousines. He followed me. I turned around to tell him to stop following me, and something struck me across the head. The next thing I know, I am here. I guess my cousin and her companion must have caught up with me and brought me here. I deeply regret that I will not see my betrothed again. He was a good man." The silence engulfed the room again as the folds of the scar stopped moving. The swelling returned, coloring it black and blue once more. The bleeding had long since stopped; clotted blood encircled the mortal blow. The inflicted gash was so deep that bone appeared to show.

The doctor didn't speak as he moved toward the lights and turned them back on. The intern was shocked by the sudden illumination and closed his eyes to shut out the bright light. He blinked and brought the doctor into focus, then looked at the patient, lying lifeless on the examination table. As he stared at her, he heard the doctor say through the glass doors to the police, "Did you get that?" Affirmatives could be heard.

The officer in charge said through the doors, "We'll issue a statement for the press. Her disappearance was a big deal. Thank you, doctor."

"My pleasure to serve, Officer Watterson."

The police turned away from the glass doors with large black letters that labeled the room as CORONER'S EXAMINATION ROOM. As they left, the intern continued to stare at the woman. For the first time, he spoke, "I wish everyone's scars could speak." The doctor moved toward the intern sympathetically. He had done well for his first field encounter. It was never easy for anyone's first time.

He shared with him experiences he hoped would help. "Son," he said to lessen the formality of the situation, "everyone's scars speak. There are two things you have to remember—one, to listen so that you can hear; and two, sometimes the scars are so deep on the inside, we are unable to see them and therefore don't listen when they do speak." The intern turned away from the beautiful woman and looked into the eyes of the doctor. For a moment, he thought he heard a faint voice.

For My Pastor

I came across a tree while weary on my journey. I had come to the end of myself, tired, beaten by the wind, seared by the sun, and exhausted from the cruel cold. The tree invited me to find rest underneath the strength of its boughs; under the cover of its leaves, in the coolness of the soil surrounding it. "I am glad you happened to be here!" I said. The tree swayed back and forth and paused as if all the moments it had seen and experienced were slowly culminating to counsel a young sapling.

The tree began, "It is not happenstance, dear one, that allows me to be here. You little know what it cost me to provide you with this comfort and respite. I was placed on earth, away from the warming rays of the sun, away from the caress of the wind, and away from the touch of all other things. In that solitude, I grew. I broke forth out of the earth, reaching toward the sun and stabilizing myself with deep roots in the earth. It wasn't over yet. In the storms of life, I had to bow so that I could continue to stand. I had to be alone as I learned to take in my environment—not to become a part of it, but for my sustenance. As I continued through the uncomfortableness of life, the rebuilding of my soil, maintaining my roots, and getting stronger to be a help to others, I am now here for you."

I looked at the tree and said, "Thank you. I'm sorry; I didn't know."

The tree responded, "It is not your apology nor your pity that I seek, but your understanding that when you see me, you do not see what it cost me to be here. It is an easy thing for you to partake of what I am now, but it was not an easy thing for me to have arrived here today."

The King's Depository

The couple waited in line as they heard a loud, booming voice say, "Lift her up and put on her royal robes. Place on her head a crown, and on her hand the ring of her father's house!"

After a pause, they heard a different, gentle voice: "Enter children." The man and woman looked at each other; they were next. Both took a deep breath and walked forward. The outside doors were so low, one almost had to stoop to enter the church. After entering, they marveled! The ceiling rose high into a dome, exhibiting sparkling lights that reflected from one wall to the other. The water in the pool shimmered underneath the lights. It was a vast room from one side to the next. The longer they looked, the larger it appeared. A woman walked past them, regal in dress, with a crown on top of her head that read *Beauty*. Looking down, they saw the altar—the reason for their visit. The woman began to shake. Her husband next to her felt the shaking and placed his hand on her shoulder, causing her to look up at him. She breathed again and was ready. They walked down to the altar, each step feeling heavier than the last. They had to make it; if they turned back this time, they wouldn't be back.

A man appeared from behind the altar and approached them. He also wore a crown that read *Redeemed*. His robe was so white, it reflected the lights from the dome above. The front of his robe read *Undershepherd*. He spoke kindly to the couple, whose eyes showed their weariness at getting there. "What is it that you would have the King do for you?" They looked at each other again, and both began to cry. This was it. They were going to leave their most prized possession with the King. The man held his wife and let her weep hard into his chest. The robed man stood by patiently. He had been here before with others who traveled this same road to arrive at this place.

After a while, the husband lifted his wife's hand and placed it on her heart. "Wait," she said with a sobbing voice. She turned to the robed man and said, "Sir, can you tell me what other precious things you have here? How do I know our deposit will be safe?" The robed man thought back on all the depositories he had seen in his life—all precious, all worth the tears of the depositor, all hard to release.

He decided to start with his most recent experience first. "A woman came here to deposit the ashes of her life. She felt like it was all she had left after making decision after decision that failed her. The King gave her a crown of beauty for her ashes." He continued, "A child deposited secret hurts that left visible scars. They received a crown of restoration." He kept going until he finished with his own story. "Years ago, I stood where you are as a young man. I didn't know there was a King who loved me. I came here and deposited my life with him. This is the one he gave me back." He allowed his last words to ebb into the silence of their thoughts.

The wife looked into her husband's eyes and reached into her heart, pulling out a small child and laying it in her husband's awaiting hands. He looked at her and nodded, then turned and spoke to the robed man, "This is our child. Our firstborn son died during my wife's pregnancy, but we didn't know. He was born still and couldn't be awakened. We have carried him in our hearts for a long time, mourning, and the weight has become too heavy for us to bear. We wish to deposit him in the King's vault. The robed man looked into the weeping eyes of the man and tenderly received the still child. With the stillborn baby in his arms, he turned to the altar. As he did, a tiny door opened. Colored light flooded out of it as he leaned forward and deposited the baby.

He closed the tiny door and turned back to the couple. They appeared to be standing straighter now. He placed his hands on their heads and called in a voice that was unlike the one he had just used; it was booming, throaty, and authoritative: "Put on them the royal robes! Place on their heads a crown and on their hands the ring of their Father's House!" From everywhere came altar workers with robes and rings and two crowns that read *Joy*. The couple was so full that they leapt around the altar. With smiles, they clasped each other's hands and walked up the aisle anew. They passed a soldier holding a triangle-folded flag. The woman smiled at the soldier and wondered if he could see it through his grief. No matter. His deposit would have him feeling lighter in just a little while.

The Treasure Box

The woman walked into her bedroom and kneeled before her bed. The early light cast beams of sunshine across it. She breathed and reached under her bed while holding her breath, then exhaled as she pulled out a humble wooden box. It was dark, medium-sized, and light to the touch, though it weighed heavily with the memories it contained. She removed the lid of the box to reveal its rich red silk lining and the contents that lay in it. Carefully and with awe, she handled her memories. The first was a seamless silk robe. It seemed out of place for her and her husband to have had a son to wear it, but he was deserving of it. Underneath it was a gold coin, given to her and her husband at her son's birth. She hugged the robe, inhaling the scent, remembering her dear son, the eldest of her children. Next, she pulled out a single thorn—it too seemed odd as a remembrance of her son, but it reminded her of his strength, his humility, and his love for his own children. He was a good man.

She gingerly placed it on the floor next to the robe and reached in for the heaviest token she coveted, a nail. It felt like fire, burning in her hands as she remembered the hollow metal sounds made as one was hammered into her son's feet. Tears filled her eyes. How could men be so cruel? How could men who handled the holy law be so injurious? The tears were now streaming as she placed it down and picked up a white swatch. Her smile ebbed the tears. Her son was alive! No matter what they did, no matter what they said, no matter what stories were circulated about Him, He was alive! "Mary?" She jumped at hearing the voice from the doorway. She didn't hear the footsteps of her visitor. "What are you doing? Are you all right?"

She closed her eyes and held the swatch in both hands before answering. "Yes. I was just thinking about my Son. I'll be ready in a moment. We can journey to see our cousin Elizabeth. She is older now, and I am sure our visit will encourage her in the passing of her husband, Zechariah. I believe John will accompany us too." Mary replaced her keepsakes gently into the humble treasure box, storing away once again a mother's love.

He's Coming

The branches swayed. The leaves rustled. The wind ebbed and flowed like an ocean as it moved from one tree to the next. The trees shook violently with the whispering message, *He's coming!* It traveled across the forest to its edge and the awaiting ears of the recipient. The preacher raised his head from attending to his garden. It was situated just beyond his cabin. The smoke willowed in the wind as it wafted from the chimney. It was early in the day for a fire, but it always made the cabin feel cozy to see the flickering light across his furniture and hear the crackling of the wood burning. He thought he heard something and looked around to see if his spouse was coming; maybe the voice was hers. He didn't see her. He called out, "Honey?" No answer. It must have been his imagination. He was lost in revelry over Sunday's message, so maybe he thought it was something.

The angel looked at the preacher from atop the cabin's roof. He sighed; the preacher still talked himself out of the supernatural. The angel looked into the distance and flew to the church down the street. He entered the pastor's study and addressed his superior, "General, the news is here. Doubt is coming; I heard the message myself as it was carried to Passivity and Anxiety at the edge of the forest, dwelling in the tarot reader's house. They have tried to attack him but don't have a strong foothold. Doubt was called in as a familiar spirit from his youth. If he isn't always right, he feels less than those he leads."

The general looked up and contemplated the intelligence he had just received. He wanted to give the angel a strategic lesson. "When Doubt speaks to him and he listens without rebuking him, say this."

The angel listened intently, "Brilliant, my general! I will do as you have said." The angel returned to his post and saw a dark figure walking toward the preacher. He was still in his garden.

"Reverend!" he said, thrusting out his hand to shake the preacher's hand. The preacher stood up and looked into the stranger's eyes while removing his gloves to shake his hand. He didn't remember seeing him at any of the services.

"Well, sir. Nice to meet you! Who might you be?"

"Sayfeck. Amallek Sayfeck. My friends call me Amal." The preacher raised an eyebrow. The name didn't fit with the countryside.

"That's quite a mouthful. Where might you be from?"

The stranger laughed. "Not from around here, as you may have noticed. It is still customary to see the preacher, the banker, and the realtor whenever one comes into town."

They both laughed at this and continued to converse.

"Can I offer you something to drink? I believe my wife made some fresh lemonade this morning."

"Thank you; no. I just stopped by to see the man who ran the church and had million-dollar dreams." The stranger laughed at these words, but it didn't feel like a joke to the preacher.

"Well, yes. We serve a big God and choose to dream big."

"I agree! I'm new in town, so maybe I missed the building fund and all the support from the town for the new church project. It's nice to have good neighbors." The stranger was saying the right things, but the preacher felt uneasy. What was he getting at? What did he really mean?

"No building fund and no support from the town. We are believing God to get the new church built."

The stranger stammered when he responded, "No building fund? No support from the town? And the project costs millions of dollars? Wow, you people don't believe in starting out small, like with an addition first until you have the funds. I thought the Bible said to count up the cost so as not to fall short and be ashamed." The preacher shifted. The stranger was still smiling, but his words evoked a familiar fight within him. Why hadn't they thought of that? It would be less stressful, and they wouldn't have to deal with a potential failure. The angel observed the poisonous words entering the spirit of the preacher. He stood beside him and looked Doubt in the face as he spoke into the ears of the preacher.

The preacher snapped and spoke words that didn't feel like they came from him: "The Bible also says that the cattle on a thousand hills belong to our God. He isn't short on resources." The preacher chuckled at the smiling stranger and noticed a slight turn in his smile. He decided to end the conversation by saying, "I'll see you in church on Sunday. Perhaps you'll stop back over to meet my wife."

The stranger looked past the preacher and spoke to the angel, "I'll most certainly be back."

Without missing a breath, the preacher responded, "We'll be waiting for you." The angel smiled as Doubt walked away. This preacher had guff!

An Unfit Counselor

She found the suite number and verified it was the correct one. On the window of the door, it read, *psychologist*. She had found this therapist through her research on the web. She checked all the boxes except one, Christian. That wasn't a deal-breaker for her because she wasn't going to her for a Sunday morning sermon or salvation. She just needed clarity on a few things in her life. She opened the door and entered the office—it was, as she expected, muted greens, hues of warm beige, and soft watercolors to calm the antagonized soul. The receptionist at the front desk took her name and bid her to sit down in one of the wingback chairs. She had her choice as the only person in the waiting room.

"Miss Copenhagen?"

The woman stirred in her seat. "Yes?"

"This way, please." The receptionist stood up from her seat to escort the woman to the office behind her. "You are expected for your appointment. Have a nice visit!"

"Thank you," the woman returned and walked past her into the office. It was immaculate! Almost the size of her living room, with homey furnishings. The exception was the desk directly in front of a large single window. The noon sun blared through it and caused the woman to place her hand over her brow as a shield from the glare.

The psychologist stood from her desk, outstretching her hand to greet her new patient warmly. "Hello! I am Athena. Thank you for coming today, Miss Copenhagen."

The new patient returned the handshake while still shielding her eyes. "Diana," she returned. "You're welcome, Dr.—"

"No need to be formal," she interrupted, "it is just Athena." The doctor turned from her new patient and closed the blinds to block the sun." She chuckled slightly and explained, "The sun is on my back, so I don't get the same glare. My apologies. Please. Take a seat; anywhere you choose." Diana looked around and saw the chaise lounge chair. It was cheesy, but she felt she could be more honest without looking into the eyes of this doctor. She wouldn't feel judged while sharing her story if she couldn't see her facial reactions.

Diana gestured toward the chaise chair. "Is this all right?"

Athena answered lightly, "Sure! Whatever makes you feel most comfortable. I'll sit alongside you, if that is okay."

"Fine." Diana sat on the lounge and swung her legs onto it so that she was comfortably sitting.

"Now," Athena began, "what brings you in to see me?"

Diana swallowed and tried to be as honest and succinct as she could without melodramatic details. "My life's dream had always been to be a wife, a mother, and a successful entrepreneur. I wanted it all for my life. I am forty-two years old and unmarried. I am involved with a man now." She hesitated.

Athena picked up on the pause. "But…what is the matter with your relationship with him?"

"I don't know exactly. He does things that seem like red flags for me to walk away, and then he is very sweet, which makes me reconsider leaving him. It even makes me consider staying to spend my life with him."

"Like what? Give me an example."

"Well," Diana started, "he asks me to do things, and if I don't do them perfectly, he yells at me and asks, Why can't I get his instructions right?"

Athena interrupted, "Has he ever hit you during these times of anger or made you feel unsafe, Diana?"

"No, never! He has acted so unkindly that I wonder if that is something I want to face in the future. I know what sets him off, but I can't help being human." Diana started to sniffle. A tissue appeared alongside her. "My friends and family tell me that our relationship isn't healthy, but he is the sweetest person when he isn't acting that way. He apologizes afterward and gives me makeup gifts. Outside of his outbursts, he is a really good man who could be a father to my children."

"Diana, it sounds like you have your thoughts clear on what you think about this area of your life. How can I help you?"

"That's just it. I'm not clear. Are my friends and family right about him? I feel like this is my last chance to start a family with a good guy, and I have to choose between what my family says and what I think." Diana looked down at her hands. They were wringing the tissue given to her by the doctor. Athena didn't rush to fill the silence left by Diana. She took her time to answer thoughtfully.

"I won't pretend to be an expert in this area. You are the expert in your life. I will share with you something to help you navigate this part of it. We should respect the observations of our loved ones and friends—many times they see red flags that we are unaware of. We must also be cognizant of their hidden biases. I'll give you an example. In my mother's time, red lipstick was all the rage. Now, a nude lip color is the fashion rage, but because of my mother's upbringing and what she was exposed to, she still chooses red. Don't mix someone else's bias with what they think is a red flag. If you believe you can make a go of this relationship and find your own happiness, my suggestion is not to hold yourself back. Remember, this is your decision."

Diana listened and felt she had a newfound courage to move forward. She was still uneasy, but the doctor's words made sense.

"I see what you mean. It is my life. I had lost track of that. Thank you, doctor."

"Athena," she corrected her. "You are welcome. It was my pleasure. I am glad you came to see me today. I am here if you would like to make another appointment to discuss this further."

Diana took the cue and swung her legs around to stand. It hadn't been very long, but she felt heavy, like she was going into a slumber. Athena escorted her to the door, ending the appointment in the same way it began: with a warm handshake. Diana left Athena to open the curtains again and let in the blocked sunlight. After repositioning herself in her chair, she heard a familiar voice coming from behind her. Destroyer floated in and called her by her given name. "Desperation, is she on the hook?"

Athena turned around and smiled. "Of course. If Anger can hold his nature for a little while longer, he will have her." Athena's smile turned into a malevolent grin. The humans made her job so easy, forgetting that their master isn't limited by time.

Failure is not an Option

The bell over the door rang, alerting the waitress to the incoming customer. She walked to the hostess's podium and greeted him. "Welcome! Will this be for here or to go?" she asked with a smile.

The customer scanned the room before answering, finding his colleague. "I'll be joining him over there." He pointed to a window booth at a man drinking a mug filled with a steaming drink.

"Yes, sir," she replied while picking up a menu to escort him to his seat. The seated man looked up at his guest and the waitress and smiled as his guest sat opposite him at the table. "I'll be back for your order," she said and walked away. She didn't like the man seated at the table. There was something about him that made her feel uncomfortable.

"So is this a business meeting, or are you here for my company?" the seated man said with sarcasm, knowing the answer already. The man looked at him across the table, smiling and withholding his anger.

"Of course, it is for your company. There's no other reason why I would be in this quiet little town with little choice for diversions." The seated man sipped from his steaming mug. His tone turned cold. "Why are you really here, Destruction?"

Destruction smiled at the sudden seriousness of the question. The cat-and-mouse game was over. He answered with a derisive smile, "The strongman wants to know how you let him slip through your fingers."

The waitress returned, interrupting the two. "Are you ready to order?"

Destruction looked up. "I'll have what he is having."

"Coffee, black? No cream or sugar?"

"Coffee, black." Destruction repeated. The waitress leaned over to pick up his menu. She could feel the other man looking at her. She turned crisply on her heels without looking at him. A few minutes later, she returned with a steaming mug of coffee and a pot of coffee to refill the seated man's cup.

"Will that be all gentlemen? Can I get you a slice of apple pie to go with your coffee?"

"No. Thanks," Destruction answered. She turned and walked back to the counter, relieved to be away from her customers.

"You were saying?" Destruction said, sipping his coffee. The seated man looked out the window, sipping his freshened cup of coffee, stubbornly refusing to answer the question or look at his company.

Destruction said sternly, "Lust. You were saying?" Lust looked up after hearing Destruction's tone. He stopped nursing his coffee to answer.

"We had him," he said flatly.

"We?" Destruction eyed Lust over his coffee mug.

"Self-righteous was assigned to him too. He was involved with a woman who wasn't right for him, brought into his circle of friends by me. He attended a virtual church service out of convenience and was going after all the eye candy he could handle—promotion at work; a large home for only himself; two cars for only himself—all to look good and because it looked good. He sacrificed study time, service time, and being around fellow believers to have what he wanted. Self-righteous convinced him he deserved it for working so hard, and I touched his eye gate to make him want it. Everything was going perfectly until he started talking to this beauty at work." Lust squeezed his mug hard at the thought, remembering his mistake.

"She seemed like a looker at first, but when we got closer to her, she didn't smell right. She carried the aroma of one who had been with the Master." He flinched at this. "I tried to steer him back to the woman I picked out for him, but he kept coming back to the one at work. Self-righteous was losing his grip in the midst of their conversations; without Self-righteous as a blind, he started seeing things differently. He started seeing himself differently. Then he went to church with her."

Destruction set his mug on the table hard, interrupting, "I've heard enough!" His face was calm, but his words cut with stabbing anger. "You two buffoons let another one escape that you had in your hands. All you geniuses had to do was to keep him occupied with everything but church and keep him away from Truth. That is it! My report will be scathing, reflecting the ineptitude of you both." Destruction cooled his tone. "If I were you, I'd get back to my human to see if I could fix this mess before the strongman reads my report." Destruction stood up to walk out the door. The waitress approached him for the bill. He looked over his shoulder at Lust. "It's on him." She looked at the seated man and returned to the counter.

Lust nursed his coffee again, watching out the window as Destruction walked to the trees and floated away. He rehearsed Destruction's last words: *If I were you, I'd get back to my human to see if I could fix this mess.* He couldn't. His human was under prayer protection. Lust wondered to himself why he was in a coffee shop instead of a bar. He then wondered if spirits could commit suicide. Maybe he could turn himself over to the enemy. Anything had to be better than what the strongman would have in store for him. A woman walked past the window with a low V-neck blouse and skin-tight trousers. Maybe he could make amends by attaching himself to another human, he thought as he watched her walk down the sidewalk. He was ready to pay the bill.

Board Meeting

The wheel on the light pole was still. No wind was blowing. It wasn't needed; it was a mild day. He hurriedly walked through the door and down the stairs to the basement. He was late. Quickly sitting in the first available chair, looking up at the picture on the wall entitled *Introduction*, it appeared he'd made it in time for the start of the briefing. The presenter stood alongside the picture, commanding the attention of the room. He spoke in a short military clip. "Gentlemen. I'm glad you could join me for this meeting today." He eyed the latecomer when he said this. He allowed the time to linger, achieving his goal of making the latecomer uncomfortable under his stare. A few minutes later, he turned his attention to the presentation. "Gentlemen, we are here to discuss our next assignment. Pay close attention to the clip. There will be a quiz at the end."

The clip played. It began with a young mother holding one child in her arm, holding the hand of another with her free arm, and walking down the street. The young mother bought diapers, returned home where she cooked lunch for the young child, and put the baby to bed. Afterward, she sat at the table with a cup of coffee and read Scriptures. The clip ended.

The presenter returned to the front of the room and addressed the audience. "Gentlemen, what have we just seen?" The room was silent. He goaded them on, "Surely, gentlemen, someone has thoughts on what we have just seen."

Arrogance spoke up, "I think we haven't seen a thing. Another young mother has children. Whoop-de-do!" A wave of chuckling washed over the room.

"Does everyone feel the same way?" the presenter asked. Heads nodded around the room. The presenter polled the eight-man room.

"Mr. Arrogance has said we saw nothing impressive. Do you feel the same way, Mr. Deception?"

"Yes."

"Mr. Lust?"

"Yes."

"Mr. Envy?"

"Yes."

"Mr. Discord?"

"Yes."

"Mr. Worry?"

"Yes."

"Mr. Hatred?"

"Yes."

"Mr. Murder?"

"Yes."

"Fools!" He exploded, suddenly changing the atmosphere. It was stern and uncomfortable. His eyes reflected his internal fury. His voice rumbled in his mouth and escaped his lips as a roar across the room. "It baffles me that our master does not throw all of you into the abyss with the other waiting beasts." His stern rebuke continued to berate the group. "You blind buffoons have missed the same principle over and over again. Even the flesh creature monkeys can learn. Must I constantly remind you of your failures? Eve: You attacked her instead of her husband. Moses: You thought he wasn't a threat in the wilderness. Samson: You pierced his eyes instead of his heart. Mary: Had you corrupted her, you would not have had to worry about her seed! Incompetents!" The presenter finished his rant and paused to allow his composure to return.

Arrogance broke the silence. "Destroyer, why is this mother different than the others?"

Destroyer breathed an audible sigh before answering. "Have I not made my point clear, Mr. Arrogance? This group underestimates the humble. You want big prey to brag about at our meetings, and you miss huge conquests before you because they are dressed differently. This 'not impressive mother' as you describe her has set a faithful example of loving her LORD in front of her children, her family, her community, and her workplace. She has exhibited a standard for the men watching her. She has a reputation for honesty in her local marketplace. Think of the great fall she represents as well as the loss of faith for those connected to her. You constantly miss the spider-web of success with your cases—your victims. You forget about the stolen future and the protected innocence of her children and their friends. You imbeciles seek glory instead of success."

The room was quiet once more. Destroyer broke the silence. "Now that I have your proper attention, we will establish our business plan to tear her down. Before we begin, I want to remind you of how to cook a frog. If you place him in boiling water, he will jump out. If you place him in comfortable water and change his environment one degree at a time, he will let you boil him alive. Now, gentlemen, let us get to work on how to boil this Christian alive!" The room roared with hails to their king. Arrogance looked at the wall again to examine the young mother. His perspective changed, and he began to relish his upcoming assignment.

Memories

"But Daddy—"

The daughter's words were cut off by her father's angry declaration, "I don't want anything to do with your God! Don't call me with this crap again!" He hung up the phone, leaving his daughter still holding her cell phone up to her ear with tears streaming down her face. She lowered her phone and began to pray for her dad.

The man laid his cell phone on the table over his bed. He looked at the television in front of him, playing nothing in particular. He jumped at the nurse's voice. "Mr. Blue, are you ready for your nightly dose?"

He rolled his head to the side to look at her and said "yes" hoarsely. Like before, she handed him a small cup with two pills. He leaned forward to place the cup on his lips and throw it back, accepting the pills. He reached for the water she had ready for him and drank both down. The nurse helped get him comfortable before leaving. Rebellion came from the room's corner, stopping alongside the father's bed. A cord was dangling from the man's heart. Rebellion picked up the cord, found the other end, and began to pull it tight, slowly. As he pulled the cord, the memories were squeezed from his heart. Rebellion clicked his tongue over his fangs. Another spirit appeared on the father's other side. It touched the father's mouth, and he began to murmur as the cord tightened. Tears alternated in his eyes.

"He'll never forgive me for the way I treated her mother." Rebellion smiled, pulling the cord tighter.

"He'll never forgive me for leaving my family." Rebellion looked at the spirit and nodded his head as he continued to pull the cord.

"He'll never forgive me for walking away from him when I was younger. I knew who God was and didn't follow Him."

"He'll never forgive me. I did it all on purpose and wanted it all."

The man continued to murmur until he had fallen asleep. Rebellion gave a last tug on the cord, causing the man to jerk in his sleep. Rebellion laughed spitefully. He looked up at Deception and winked. "Good work! I was convinced the enemy wouldn't forgive him after listening to that."

They both laughed wickedly while Deception complimented himself, "I'll be a lying spirit in his mouth. I know how to do my job well." He stopped smiling and asked, "What was that cord you were pulling?"

"It was a barbed cord wrapped around his heart. As I tightened it, it pierced his heart, releasing his memories. Your touch on his lips skewed them into untruth."

"You mean he didn't mistreat his daughter's mother? Man, I'm good!"

Rebellion cackled, "Oh, he did that all right; but he hasn't done anything that can't be forgiven. That was the untruth."

A voice wafted in the breeze through the window. *God, I pray a hedge of protection around my father, and I pray Your truth be revealed to him.* Angels entered the room as if attached to the breeze, surrounding the father and pushing Rebellion and Deception away from the man. The angels encircled the father, standing with swords out. Rebellion and Deception looked at each other. They didn't pull their swords; instead, they wafted backward, up out of the hospital room, staring at their enemies as they stood stone-faced, ready for any resistance.

They perched themselves on the branches overhanging the hospital building, watching as the nurse reentered the man's room. "Mr. Blue. Are you all right? I heard you talking in your sleep again." An angel turned inward toward the man as the others tightened the gap he had left. He touched the man's heart, removing the remnants of the poisonous cord.

"I'm not sure. I...I..." He stammered while another figure appeared behind the nurse. He was clothed in all black, holding a Bible.

"Mr. Blue. Is it okay if I come in to speak with you?" The man looked past the nurse, seeing a clerical collar on the figure.

"Yes!" Mr. Blue brightened. I think I would like to speak with you." The nurse turned around to see the chaplain. She smiled and walked away to leave them to talk privately.

Mr. Blue spoke honestly. "I want to make my peace with God before I leave here, but, Chaplain, I don't think I can." Mr. Blue began weeping.

The chaplain sat on the side of the bed. "Mr. Blue, I want to share some truths with you that I think will help you." He opened the Bible and started with the truth that Mr. Blue was made in the image of God and redeemed by Him.

Rebellion and Deception watched the scene from their tree branches: a soul encamped about by angels with a man of God sharing the truth of Christ. They shrieked loudly in disgust and anger, flying away at the speed of defeat.

Class is in Session

The classroom came to attention at the appearance of the professor. "Today, class," he began, "we have the rare opportunity to learn from one of this college's most prestigious educators. Please make him feel welcome." The spirit wafted in on a bed of cold air, charging the atmosphere. The students knew who this was; no name was necessary, though he was known by many—Ayruum, Seducer, NaKash Serpent—but he preferred simply ShehKer. He held up an ornate black box with spiked horns that adorned the lid. The large screens portraying his image showed the fine detail of crimson hinges on either side of the box.

"Class, Professor Destroyer informed me that you are currently studying persuasion and how to utilize its power over humans."

"Yes, sir!" Pride yelled out, wanting the attention of this important figure. Perhaps he'll remember him for future encounters.

Professor ShehKer ignored the uncouth exclamation from the immature spirit. "I have another weapon for you to add to your arsenal." ShehKer opened the box, slowly tilting it forward for the room to see. Consumption was not impressed. He had seen this "weapon" before and made use of it himself. He immediately raised his hand. "Yes," ShehKer said knowingly.

"Professor, how will a human tongue for eating and drinking help us persuade humans? ShehKer had heard this before from inexperienced spirits and was ready for it.

"I'll show you." He removed the tongue from the box and held it out in front of himself. He turned it slightly, and it turned bright red, bursting into flames. The students leaned forward with great interest. He turned it slightly again, and it ceased burning, turning green and dripping venomous liquid from its underside. The students were beginning to be amazed. He turned it yet again, and it turned blue with icicles hanging from it.

"Students," he said as he continued to turn the tongue slightly, causing it to change into different forms of itself. "The human tongue is one of your greatest allies of persuasion. It causes destruction from within. My greatest victory came from adding one word to Eve's speech, and she bought it. She believed the lie she repeated to herself!" He chuckled with pride at this recollection. "You can cause the human to become angry at nothing with just a few implanted words; you can cause them to become murderous with their speech by twisting a part of the story; and you can cause them to become cold toward one another by omitting a few details."

He smiled with sinister satisfaction as he remembered the exploits connected to each example. He continued, becoming inflated by his own memories. "Just as I showed you with the tongue, subtly turn their words. If you are too blatant with what you implant, humans will dismiss it as a wild thought. If you embed a few inconspicuous, unimportant words, they slip past them and change the meaning enough for them to accept the deception and succumb to it. Even more beautiful is that they continue to perpetuate it without your further investment of energy or influence, freeing you to work on another area of their lives. By the time you are finished, they are in bondage to a web without realizing they spun it themselves. That is when you bring in Mr. Pride to put an additional hold on them, preventing them from turning to Truth for their freedom." Pride perked up at being recognized. The bell sounded.

"Students, show your appreciation to our prestigious guest for that most excellent presentation!"

The room broke out in applause. He was brilliant! Laptops closed, feet shuffled, and students hurried through the door, enthused at the thought of trying their new method of destruction.

I Know Her

The devil came for me. I sensed his presence, noticed his tricks, recognized his tactics, and rebuked him. I resisted him and commanded him out of my atmosphere. Unable to get to me himself, he sent a familiar seducer, a familiar face, a once-known usurper. I was not on guard. I allowed my enemy to walk up to me without resistance or obstacles. I looked into the eyes of my enemy and consented to everything she told me. I let her seduce me into leaning toward the right when I should have gone left. Why did I listen to her! She came for me when he couldn't get close to me. I listened to her when I silenced him. I embraced her when I pushed him away. I had a conversation with her when I wouldn't even take his calls. He sent a clever enemy. When I saw her, I allowed myself to be captured—nearly without resistance, nearly surrendering. She slowly walked me into the territory of my real enemy, and I came along, sometimes beside her, sometimes following, but always away from my God. He attacked me with my habits; he attacked me with me, and I succumbed to my own efforts. My old man's nature returned, and I sabotaged me. The devil found a confederate in my old man, and he was willing to capture an old enemy to return to her old way of life. I won't stop me. I renounce my old self, that old woman. Long may she die!

Bed Shopping

I hate bed shopping for me, let alone for someone else. The decision seems so final. One decision for what seems like an eternity. I mean, I know what I like, but what do they like for themselves? It's one thing to share a bed that is already present, but to buy a new one is a different matter. Would they like a firm bed or a softer bed? A fluffy pillowtop that props the head up or one that allows it to lay straight back? Which one looks better? I like to lay on my side, moving from one side to the other throughout the night. What do you get for a sedentary sleeper? I think he might prefer comfort over firmness.

Now, the color is another matter. They make so many these days, it's hard to choose. I like bright and pastel; of course, I wouldn't pick that for him, so he can roll over and say something to me about it. No way! I'll stay neutral and do a soft white—something we both can agree upon. While part of my family is celebrating a joyous graduation, I'm here. Alone. It's not as jubilant as a graduation, but it does allow contemplative time. Like conversations that we once had, pillow talk. Or, times when the silence was so loud, it screamed what neither one of us refused to say to one another. It also causes one to lose track of time while standing over the bed.

"Ma'am?" I hear. "You have made an excellent choice! This model is trimmed in gold, has a pillowtop, and will allow the occupant comfort. It is also durable and comes with a warranty. We are very proud of that fact. If you would follow me to the office, I can provide you with more details, and we can discuss price points for different amenities."

"Sure," I hear myself reply, standing over the model, which represents my final decision. "I'm sure my husband would find this suitable as well."

"Yes ma'am! It is one of our most popular models. This is one of our top-of-the-line caskets."

"Yes," I continue to answer as if not hearing the salesman, "this bed will suit my husband just fine. He will rest well in it."

The Gift

I love gifts! Especially ones I wasn't expecting. It's like having a mini surprise birthday party. Someone or a group of people thought so much of you that they expressed it tangibly. I didn't know I was going to receive this gift bag—beautifully dressed with alternating black and white contrasting tissue paper arranged in a black ornate bag. Very eye-catching. It's an honor to receive it out of all the people here that it could have been given to. Honor isn't supposed to bring sorrow, is it? So why has it?

I smile as I receive this bag of unknown treasures, but really, I don't feel like smiling. I don't feel like being here. I don't feel like feeling. Forget about wearing a mask to hide my feelings; I feel like I'm wearing a full helmet to shield my emotions. Emotions that, if they could, would give back this gift bag and rewind the clock. Emotions that would have me standing up on a chair in the middle of the room and gladly "bestowing" this honor on another. But when it's your gift, it belongs to you. This is one of those gifts that can't be regifted. "Thank you," I say as the young, suited man hands me the gift bag. "What's in it?"

"It has the sign-in registry and additional obituaries from your grandmother's service as well as other items."

"Oh, thank you." Those are the polite words to say, the appropriate words to say, but not the words I want to say. The silence, the darkness, and my Lord will hear those. I look at it again; the beautifully ornate bag has the logo of the funeral company on it. I won't get this bag mixed up with any of the other consolatory gifts I received. I place the bag in the trunk of my father's car and nestle it among the plants that once sat around my grandmother in front of the church. I looked into it. The picture of my grandmother looks back at me with twinkling eyes, braided hair, and a bright smile, all motionless. No, I won't mix this gift up with any of the others.

About the Author

Ms. Miller is a native of Ohio. She resides there with her family, where she covets her title of "great aunt." She is also a Christian education teacher, serves on multiple boards, and is a proud civil servant. As a lifelong learner, among her loves is Bible teaching, where a great deal of her inspiration comes from for her stories. She wrote informally in college and continued throughout her personal life. She is an avid volunteer at her church and plans to continue her growth there. She describes her style of writing as "connections to the word of God in her heart." She is a proud believer. Her aim is to strive for what God has for her and live to the fullest by doing God's will by serving others in her daily walk. She believes that everyone has a story, and people's lives are the culmination of many steps. Robin Miller can be found on YouTube, Facebook, and Instagram.